MOTHER GOOSE & MORE
CLASSIC RHYMES with ADDED LINES

ADDITIONS BY
Dr. Hickey

PICTURES BY
Marissa Moss

LIBRARY OF CONGRESS CATALOGING-IN-PUBLICATION DATA

Dr. Hickey, 1909- .   Mother Goose & More: Classic rhymes with added lines /
additions by Dr. Hickey; pictures by Marissa Moss.   p.   cm.
Summary: A collection of traditional nursery rhymes,
each of which has new lines added to it.
ISBN 0-9623940-0-9
1. Children's poetry, American. 2. Nursery rhymes. [1. Nursery rhymes.
2. American poetry.] I. Moss, Marissa, ill. II. Mother Goose. III. Title.
IV. Title: Mother Goose and More.   89-36000
PS3558.I227M68   1990   CIP
811' .54--dc20   AC

These rhymes are dedicated to
Siddie Jo Johnson
and to my family

The original Mother Goose verses are in black ink.

The additions by Dr. Hickey are in blue.

C O N T E N T S

Humpty Dumpty

Humpty Dumpty sat on a wall.
Humpty Dumpty had a great fall.
All the King's horses and all the King's men
Couldn't put Humpty together again.

They called a doctor from the town
To come and fix poor Humpty's crown.
He put a stitch in Humpty's leg
And bandaged up poor Humpty's egg.

He used some tape and then some glue,
And Humpty's now as good as new.

11

School Time

A diller, a dollar
A ten o'clock scholar,
What makes you come so soon?
You used to come at ten o'clock
And now you come at noon.

The summer sun
Did make me run
Before the hour of noon.
In winter when it's cold outside,
I don't wake up so soon.

My Son John

Diddle diddle dumpling, my son John,
Went to bed with his stockings on.
One shoe off and one shoe on,
Diddle diddle dumpling, my son John.

Diddle diddle dumpling, one shoe fell.
Off came the stockings and pants as well.
Time to put pajamas on,
Diddle diddle dumpling, my son John.

13

The Pussycat Song

Pussycat, pussycat,
Where have you been?
    I've been to London
    To visit the Queen.

Pussycat, pussycat,
What did you there?
    I frightened a little mouse
    Under her chair.

Pussycat, pussycat,
Was the King told?
    Yes, for my mousing
    He gave me some gold.

Pussycat, pussycat,
What did you then?
    I bowed to the Queen
    And came home again.

Hickety Pickety

Hickety pickety, my black hen,
She lays eggs for gentlemen.
Gentlemen come every day
To see what my black hen doth lay.
Sometimes nine and sometimes ten,
Hickety pickety, my black hen.

But hickety pickety, my black hen
Sometimes lays few eggs and then
The gentlemen are very sad.
But on some days, the laying's bad.
And when they ask me why or when,
I tell them, please ask my black hen.

Then she says give me lots of corn,
And come for your eggs upon the morn.

Do Beggars Have a King?

Hark, hark
The dogs do bark.
The beggars are coming to town.

Some in rags
And some in tags
And one in a red velvet gown.

Is he the king?
With a bright golden ring?
Does he rule the beggars in town?

No, he plays the fiddle,
Sings hey diddle diddle,
And walks on his hands upside-down.

17

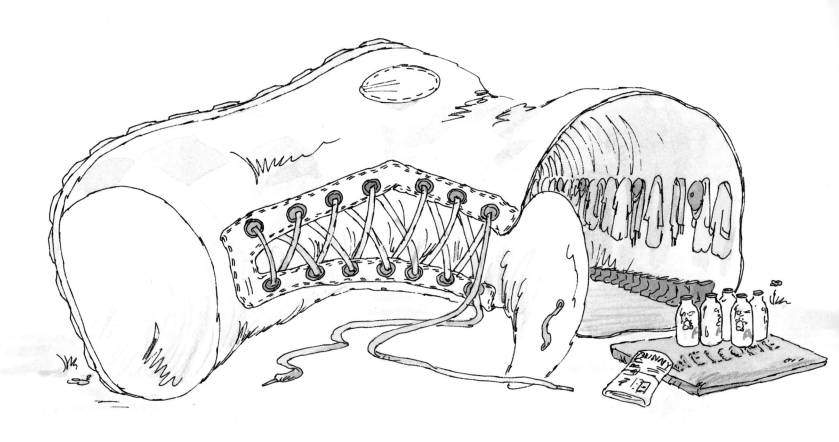

The Old Woman Who Lived in the Shoe

There was an old woman
Who lived in a shoe.
She had so many children
She didn't know what to do.

She gave them some broth
Without any bread.
She whipped them all soundly
And sent them to bed.

But early next morning,
As children awake,
She gave each a breakfast
Of sweet milk and cake.

And then the old woman
Without a delay
Just kissed them all fondly
And sent them to play.

Jack a Dandy

Handy spandy, Jack a dandy
Loves plum cake and sugar candy.
Stole some from a grocer's shop
And out he came, hop hop skip hop.

The grocer ran out shouting, "Stop!"
As Jack came skipping from the shop.
The cake was squishy-squashed and crummy.
The candy was inside Jack's tummy.

Curly Locks

Curly Locks, Curly Locks,
Will you be mine?
You shall not wash dishes
Nor yet feed the swine.

But sit on a cushion
And sew a fine seam
And feed upon strawberries,
Sugar and cream.

Curly Locks, Curly Locks,
Will you marry me?
We'll have lots of puppies,
At least two or three.

Curly Locks, Curly Locks,
You say we're too small?
We'll hurry and grow up
In no time at all!

Hey Diddle Diddle

Hey diddle diddle
The cat and the fiddle
The cow jumped over the moon.
The little dog laughed
To see such sport
And the dish ran away with the spoon.

The fork and the knife
Were humming a tune,
A salt and pepper fable.
The cat and the dog
Grabbed the knife and the fork,
And sat themselves down at the table.

They sat there for lunch.
They sat there for dinner.
They sat there the whole day through.
But there was no pie,
No milk, no cream,
Not even a biscuit or two.

No meat, no bread, not even a little,
So back they went to their hey diddle diddle.

23

Nimble Jack

Jack be nimble,
Jack be quick,
Jack jump over the candlestick.

When you reach
The other side,
Bow three times
And fetch a bride.

Be she pretty,
Be she shy,
Marry her before you cry.

Be she ugly,
Be she slow,
Jump right back
And away she'll go.

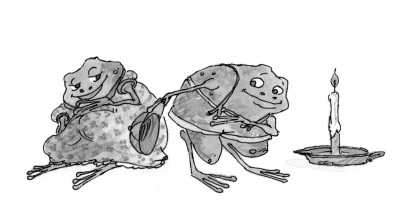

The Tale of the Barber

Barber, barber, shave a pig.
How many hairs will make a wig?

Four and twenty, that's enough.
Give the barber a pinch of snuff.

Barber, make a wig for me,
The grandest wig the world could see.

Shave a cow and I'll give you
Another pinch of snuff or two.

Dear Mother Hubbard

Old Mother Hubbard
Went to her cupboard
To get her poor dog a bone.
But when she got there
The cupboard was bare,
And so the poor dog had none.

The poor hungry dog
Tried to chew on a log,
Not a crumb, not a crust on the ground.
But dear Mother Hubbard
Again searched the cupboard
And what do you think she found?

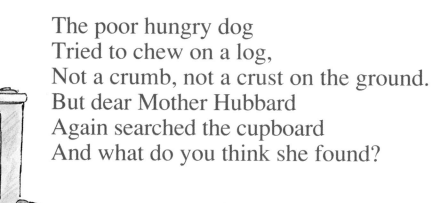

26

Way deep in the back,
In a shadow quite black,
Were biscuits she'd baked the day past.
The hungry dog ate,
And he licked clean the plate.
His tummy was filled up at last.

Mother H. won't forget
Her poor hungry pet.
On her list, she wrote: "Food for my dog."

27

Dr. Fell

I do not like thee, Dr. Fell.
The reason why I cannot tell.
But this I know and know full well,
I do not like thee, Dr. Fell.

My Mother says you'll make me well,
But that's my problem Dr. Fell.
To show my throat I'll open wide
And you may feel my back and side.

But don't expect to make me well,
Though you may try, dear Dr. Fell.
Mother thinks I'm really sick,
But this is just my stay-home trick.

28

Pins and Needles

See a pin and pick it up,
All the day you'll have good luck.

See a pin and leave it lie,
And sure you'll want before you die.

See a needle, pick it up,
On pie and honey you will sup.

See a needle, leave it lie,
And 'fore the day's out you will cry.

Little Boy Blue

Little Boy Blue come blow your horn.
The sheep's in the meadow, the cow's in the corn.
But where is the little boy tending the sheep?
He's under the haystack fast asleep.

30

Will you wake him?
   No, not I,
   For if I do, he's sure to cry.

The sheep baa baa,
   The cows moo moo,
   And wake up sleeping little Boy Blue.

So up from the haystack jumps little Boy Blue,
For shepherds can't sleep when there's work to do.
Looking high, looking low, the sheep are found.
Boy Blue leads them home all safe and sound.

Contrary Mary

Mary, Mary quite contrary
How does your garden grow?
    With silver bells and cockle shells
    And pretty maids all in a row.

Mary Mary quite contrary
Where does your garden grow?
    Way out back, near a sweet haystack
    Where I weed and I water and hoe.

Mary Mary quite contrary
You cry when the winter winds blow.
    I'll change my tune in May or June
    When it's warm and my flowers will grow.

Fat Jack Spratt

Jack Spratt could eat no fat.
His wife could eat no lean.
And so betwixt the two of them
They licked the platter clean.

Jack Spratt grew big and fat.
His wife grew thin and lean.
And still betwixt the two of them
They licked the platter clean.

Jack could get no fatter.
His wife could get no leaner.
And betwixt the two of them
The platter got no cleaner.

A Crooked Life

There was a crooked man and he walked a crooked mile.
He found a crooked sixpence against a crooked stile.
He bought a crooked cat which caught a crooked mouse
And they all lived together in a little crooked house.

34

He had a crooked wife
Who cooked a crooked fish.
She set it on a crooked table
In a crooked dish.

Crooked wife, crooked man, crooked cat, crooked mouse
Sat and ate their dinner in their little crooked house.

Sleepy Time

The cat sat asleep by the side of the fire.
The mistress snored loud as a pig.
John took up the fiddle at Jenny's desire
And struck up a bit of a jig.

The music awoke the cat bye and bye,
The mistress awoke after that.
John fiddled and Jenny sang sweetly and high,
While the mistress danced 'round with the cat.

They danced and they sang tune after tune,
Till the sun set and up came the moon.

To a Beautiful Lady Bug

Lady bug, lady bug,
Fly away home.
Your house is on fire,
Your children will burn.

They've all flown away
Except little Ann,
For she's crept under
The frying pan.

Lady bug, lady bug,
Hurry back home.
Your children all need you
And Ann's home alone.

Then build a new house
With honey and charm,
Kiss your sweet children
And keep them from harm.

Little Old Woman

There was an old woman tossed in a blanket
Seventeen times as high as the moon.
But where she was going no mortal could tell,
For under her arm, she carried a broom.

"Old woman, old woman, old woman," said I,
"Whither, ah whither, ah whither so high?"
  "To sweep the cobwebs from the sky
  And I'll be with you by and by."

The sky is swept, the clouds are clean.
No dusty cobwebs to be seen.
And who can we thank for this lovely day?
The little old woman, for now we can play!

The Tale of the Pumpkin

Peter, Peter, Pumpkin eater
Had a wife and couldn't keep her.
Put her in a pumpkin shell
And there he kept her very well.

But Peter led a lonely life.
The days were long without his wife.
He wanted her back by his side.
So off he went to fetch his bride.

He moved her from the pumpkin shell
And learned to treat her very well.
And now they're happy as can be,
Peter, his wife, and their sons three.

My Moppet is a Doll

I had a little moppet,
I put her in my pocket
And fed her with corn and hay.

There came a proud beggar,
And swore he would have her,
And stole my little moppet away.

He put my little moppet
Into his jacket pocket
And whistled as he walked on his way.

But his pocket had a hole
Through which my moppet stole
And back to me she ran so we could play.

Yankee Doodle

Yankee doodle went to town
Riding on a pony,
Stuck a feather in his cap
And called it macaroni.

Yankee rode right to the square.
He stopped to see the sights:
Some dancing bears, some bright red pears,
Dozens of delights.

He pulled the feather from his cap
To use it as a comb,
Then turned his pony right around
And rode it straight back home.

Wee Willie Winkie

Wee Willie Winkie
Runs through the town,
Upstairs and downstairs
In his nightgown.

Rapping at the window,
Calling at the lock,
"Are the children in their beds?
For now it's eight o'clock."

But why is Willie Winkie
Running through the night?
He wishes he could find a friend
To play with him tonight.

43

Ride a Cock Horse

Ride a cock horse
To Banbury Cross
To see a fine lady
Upon a white horse.

Rings on her fingers
And bells on her toes,
She shall have music
Wherever she goes.

44

The lady's a queen.
Her horse is quite grand.
They ride here and there
Throughout the whole land.

Now hurry, cock horse,
We've miles to go
From Banbury Cross,
And you're rocking so slow.